Chicks Rock!

STORY BY
Sudipta Bardhan-Quallen

PICTURES BY
Renée Kurilla

Abrams Books for Young Readers • New York

Nerdy chicks can study

Wordy chicks can talk

Soccer chicks can
take their kicks

And Rocker Chick
can ROCK!

Cooped up in her crib
This chick belts out the tunes
She strums, she drums, she hits the chords
She warbles and she croons

Music is her passion
She shreds on her guitar
She dreams it is her destiny
To be a superstar

One morning, bright and early
There is a *KNOCK KNOCK KNOCK*
It is an invitation
That leaves the rocker shocked!

Rocker Chick is gleeful

I'll make those chicks run wild!

STUFF STUFF

SONGS

She struts off to the festival
To show the world her style

She gets to dress rehearsal
Prepared to *bawk* 'n' roll

But then she sees the blinding lights
And starts to lose control

She trembles in the wings
She wonders for the first time
What if I can't sing?

Like poultry in slow motion
She climbs the backstage stairs
From there, she sees that all her peeps
Have filled the front-row chairs

The chicks are watching hopefully
She doesn't have a choice

She has to get back on that stage
And *somehow* find her voice

She walks into the spotlight
Before the microphone
Her friends are all prepared to cheer
But she feels all

ALONE

The plucky chicks begin to work
And form a master plan

Pop Chick teaches dance moves

Punk Chick picks her dress

Artsy Chick does makeup

Zen Chick helps with stress

Coding Chick plans lighting

Hippie Chick advises

Nerdy Chick writes out the set

While Cool Chick supervises

Her peeps have faith in Rocker Chick
Which helps her grow more certain
They give advice, support, and praise—
Then point her toward the curtain

At long last, it is showtime
The audience is squawking
Rocker Chick announces

But then, for just moment
The stage fright reappears
And so the chicks remind her

Rocker Chick, we're here!

She warbles out a ballad

Then drops
the sickest beats

When she plays the Chicken Dance
The crowd is on their feet

The show's a real barn burner
The fan chicks shout for more!
Rocker Chick calls up her peeps
To sing in the encore

They play the closing notes
And take a final bow

The chicks chirp,

Rocker Chick's a star!

She can't deny it now!

The chicks depart the festival
In step and wing in wing
Believing with each other's help
They can do ANYTHING!

you are going to rock the world!
—S. B. Q.

For Jen Rofé, a chick who most definitely rocks
—R. K.

This book was sketched, penciled, and painted entirely in Adobe Photoshop.

Cataloging-in-Publication Data has been applied for and
may be obtained from the Library of Congress.

ISBN 978-1-4197-4570-6

Printed and bound in China
10 9 8 7 6 5 4 3 2 1

Abrams Books for Young Readers are available at special discounts when
purchased in quantity for premiums and promotions as well as fundraising or
educational use. Special editions can also be created to specification.
For details, contact specialsales@abramsbooks.com or the address below.

Abrams® is a registered trademark of Harry N. Abrams, Inc.

ABRAMS The Art of Books
195 Broadway, New York, NY 10007
abramsbooks.com

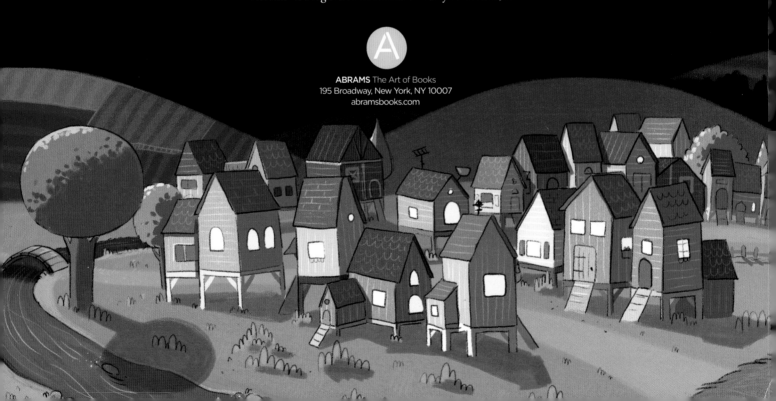